⑩

CASEBUSTERS

Sabotage on the Set

Disney Adventures

CASEBUSTERS ⑩

Sabotage on the Set

By Joan Lowery Nixon

Disney PRESS

New York

For Carol Ann Schmitz in friendship
—J. L. N.

Printed in the United States of America.

First Edition
1 3 5 7 9 10 8 6 4 2

Library of Congress Catalog Card Number: 96-86050
ISBN: 0-7868-4087-0 (pbk.)

S EAN QUINN SLAMMED the back door as he dashed into the kitchen. "Mom!" he yelled. "I'm going to be rich! Rich *and* famous!"

"Sean! Where have you been?" Mrs. Quinn put down the phone. "I was about to start calling your friends to try to find you."

Brian and his best friend, Sam Miyako, looked at each other, then back at Sean.

"What do you mean, rich and famous?" Brian asked.

Sam said, "Mrs. Quinn, now that Brian and

I don't have to go out hunting for Sean, could I please have more cookies?"

Mrs. Quinn pushed the cookie jar toward Sam, but her attention was on Sean. "Well?" she asked him. "Why didn't you come right home after school? Where were you?"

Sean tugged his backpack off, dropped it on the floor, and flopped into the nearest kitchen chair. "I told you, Mom. I'm going to be rich. Wow! Think of all the baseball cards I can buy!"

"Mom just asked where you were, not what kind of wild daydreams you're having," Brian said. He got up and started toward the back door, but Sean stopped him.

"Wait. I'll tell you all about it," he said. "Some big movie company is going to make a movie right here in Redoaks."

Sam raised an eyebrow and looked mysterious. "Not with the jinx, they won't."

Sean ignored Sam. "The movie's called *New Guy in Town*, and guess who's starring in it? Dakota Wayne! And Justin Moore!"

"Dakota Wayne? Cool," Brian said.

"Everybody knows who Dakota Wayne is," Sam said. "He's famous. But who's Justin Moore?"

"I know who he is," Brian said. "When he was five he was the coach's son on that TV show *Our Family Tree*."

"Yeah, but he's nine now—the same age as me," Sean said and grinned. "Some people who said they were casting directors for *New Guy in Town* came to our school today and visited our class. They said they wanted some of us to be extras, but they kept staring at me. Then they measured to see how tall I was, and they said I had the right coloring and height and weight and all that stuff, and . . . and . . ."

Sean took a deep breath, and in a rush of words said, "And they want me to be Justin Moore's stand-in! And they'll pay me! Can I, Mom? Can I?"

"You'd get more money if you were Dakota Wayne's stand-in," Sam said. "All those Save Joey movies made him famous."

Brian chuckled. "Sean would have a hard time being a stand-in for Dakota Wayne. Dakota's fourteen now and tall. Tiffany said that Dakota has grown so much, they only use extra-tall actors around him to make him look shorter."

"Who's Tiffany?" Mrs. Quinn asked.

Sam snickered, and Brian felt his face grow warm. "Uh, she's just a source of information," he said. "Tiffany reads movie magazines and knows all that movie stuff."

Sean leaned toward his mother. "Mom, Mom, Mom! You didn't answer. The casting director is going to call you tonight. Could I please, please take the job?"

"Sean, you know I'll have to talk this over with your father," Mrs. Quinn said. "There's a great deal we'll need to know. Will your job on the movie interfere with your schoolwork? Will one of us have to supervise you on the set? What will your working hours be?"

Sam interrupted. "And will the weird jinx on the movie put Sean in any danger?"

Everyone stopped talking and looked at Sam.

Sam didn't say anything.

Finally, Brian asked, "What weird jinx?"

"I told you about it before. I thought nobody was interested."

"We're interested. C'mon, Sam. What's the jinx you're talking about?"

"I thought everybody knew about the jinx," Sam said. "Tiffany should stop reading movie magazines and listen to that movie enter-tainment show on television."

"Sam!" Brian threatened.

"Okay, okay," Sam said. "The way I heard it was, some people in Hollywood are saying that *New Guy in Town* will never be made. The director began his career with some real block-buster hits, but lately he's had a run of flops, so he's counting on Dakota Wayne's popularity to bring this one off. Only . . ."

Sam paused until Sean demanded, "Only *what*?"

"Only, right from the beginning they've had trouble," Sam said. "There were a lot of arguments about the script, and the head scriptwriter quit. Then a Hollywood set for *New Guy in Town* was destroyed in a fire. An expensive camera fell over and was smashed. Another was stolen. Props disappeared."

"Good gracious!" Mrs. Quinn exclaimed.

"Yeah," Sam said. "So they moved the whole thing up here to Redoaks to film on location."

"Who are the people making the movie?" Mrs. Quinn asked.

"Donner Productions," Mr. Quinn answered as he walked into the kitchen. "It smells great in here. What's for dinner?"

"Dad! You're home!" Sean yelled and jumped to his feet. "I'm going to be rich and famous—that is, if you and Mom let me."

"Hey, you're good, Mr. Quinn," Sam said. "You know practically everything that's going on in Redoaks. Is that because you're a private investigator?"

Mr. Quinn laughed. "It just so happens that I was getting some information I needed at the police station, and a number of officers were signing up to work as off-duty security on the set," he said. "I heard all about the movie. The story deals with a New York City kid whose father moves his family to a small town. The boy misses his friends and can't adjust until, through his little brother, he discovers the real meaning of friendship. Frank Hightower's a good director, so it could be a very successful family movie."

"If it's made," Sam said. "You know . . . the jinx."

"Jinxes are nothing but superstitions," Mr. Quinn said. "We don't believe in jinxes." He opened the oven and glanced inside, taking a deep breath. "*Mmm*, lasagna."

"Ten more minutes until it's ready," Mrs. Quinn said. "Sam, would you like to stay for dinner?"

"Thanks," Sam said. "I was hoping you'd ask."

"Sean, suppose you set the table," Mrs. Quinn said.

"But, Mom, I've got to tell Dad about—"

"Later," she said firmly. As she took a mixed-greens salad out of the refrigerator, she added, "You'll have plenty of time to tell him during dinner."

Sean tugged a stack of plates from the cupboard and arranged them around the table. "Mom, I've just got to be Justin Moore's stand-in, no matter what."

"No matter what?" Sam made his voice low and scary. "Don't tell me you're not even a little bit afraid of the jinx?"

2

A S SOON AS PLATES HAD been passed around and everyone had begun eating, Sean burst out with his news. "The casting director is going to call tonight," Sean said. "You and Mom have got to let me take the job! Please, Dad!"

Mrs. Quinn's forehead wrinkled with concern, but Mr. Quinn said, "The school board had planned to meet today to discuss the requests by Donner Productions. Donner wants to film some of the scenes on the Redoaks Elementary School grounds. I'm sure the school board will set up regulations regarding the education of the children who'll work in the film. And there are California state laws to follow, as well, so there'll be studio teachers on hand."

"I have some questions about letting Sean take the job," Mrs. Quinn said. "It's bound to disrupt his regular studies."

Mr. Quinn smiled at Sean. "His grades have been very good. I'm sure we won't have to worry about them slipping during the two or three weeks that Donner Productions will be filming in Redoaks. The studio teachers will see to that."

"Dad's right!" Sean said, wondering if the studio teachers were tougher than Mrs. Jackson. "I'll study harder than ever."

"It might turn out to be a valuable learning experience," Mr. Quinn said.

"Yeah, Dad!" Sean said.

"And I think we'll all agree that ninety percent of what Sean earns will go into his college fund."

Sean looked at his father and gulped. There went his dreams of becoming a big-time spender. "Uh—okay, Dad," Sean said.

"All right," Mrs. Quinn said. "If you think it's the right thing to do, John, then I'll agree."

The telephone rang, and Sean jumped, dropping a glob of lasagna onto his lap.

Mrs. Quinn answered and in a few moments said, "Carol Carter? Oh, yes. The casting director. Sean said you'd call."

Everyone at the table grew silent, listening intently. But Sean squirmed and fidgeted while his mother asked one question after another. Finally, she said, "Very well. We'll have him there on time."

Sean gave a humongous sigh and blissfully slid down in his chair.

"The entire junior high basketball team will be extras?" Mrs. Quinn asked, then said, "Yes, if Brian would like to work as an extra, we'll sign for him, too."

Brian and Sam grinned at each other and slapped a high five. "Tiffany was right," Brian said. "She told me they were going to surround Dakota Wayne with guys taller than he is."

"Who's Tiffany?" Mr. Quinn asked.

Brian winced. "Uh, just a girl," he said.

As Mrs. Quinn finished the conversation and hung up the phone, Sean and Brian pelted her with questions.

"When do they start filming the movie?"

"Do extras get paid, too?"

"What was all that stuff about the basketball team?"

"Dad said two or three weeks. Do we have to go to school at all?"

Mrs. Quinn laughed and waved her hands for quiet. "Sam, you might as well get in on all this," she said. "You're on the basketball team, so you and Brian and the others are going to be extras, if your parents give permission. And, yes. Extras get paid by the day."

"How much?" Sam asked.

"You'll have to find that out from your parents," Mrs. Quinn said. "Carol Carter will be telephoning them this evening."

Sam scrambled to his feet. "Please excuse me, and thanks for dinner, Mrs. Quinn. I'd stay and help with the dishes, but ... uh ... you know."

Sean yelled after him, "Oh, yeah? When did you *ever* help with the dishes?" But Sam had already shot out the back door and was on the way to his house, next door.

Mr. Quinn chuckled. "Sam seems to have forgotten all about that so-called jinx."

"Sam was just trying to scare Sean," Brian said.

Mrs. Quinn sighed. "I wish Sam wouldn't always come up with those awful, scary stories," she said.

"Aw, Mom," Sean said. "I'm not scared of any old jinx." But even though he tried to sound brave, he felt cold prickles up his backbone. He'd never run into a jinx before, and he wasn't sure he knew how to handle it.

* * *

THE NEXT MORNING, as he entered his fourth-grade class, Sean stopped worrying about the movie jinx. He had his own horrible, scary jinx—Debbie Jean Parker.

She waved a paper in his face and said, "Sign here, and you can be a member of the Redoaks Dakota Wayne Fan Club. I'm the president, of course."

"Who elected you?" Sean asked.

"I elected myself." Debbie Jean held out her arms and tried a ballet twirl, nearly falling into the nearest desk. She caught her balance, shrugged, and said proudly, "I was signed as one of the extras. You know what that means, don't you?"

"The casting director lost her glasses," Sean said.

Debbie Jean ignored him and burbled, "It means that all of Hollywood will see my face and talent on the screen. I'll be discovered and made a star!"

"Oh, yuck," Sean said.

"And I'll actually get to meet Dakota Wayne!"

The bell rang, and Mrs. Jackson clapped her hands. "Take your seats, boys and girls. I know you're all excited about the movie that's going to be filmed here—especially those of you who are going to be in it—but we've got lots of work to do. It's time to get busy."

Sean couldn't resist temptation. As Debbie Jean was turning to go to her seat, Sean grabbed her arm and said, "You may be an extra in a few scenes in the movie, but I'm going to work as Justin Moore's stand-in."

Debbie Jean's eyes widened, and her mouth fell open.

Sean slid into his seat with a big grin on his face. This whole movie experience was going to be even more fun than he had imagined. What could go wrong? Nothing!

3

THERE WAS ANOTHER interview, and forms for Mrs. Quinn to sign. Finally, Sean was told to report to his school, and from there to the outdoor set near the east door.

"We want to see you bright and early," Miss Carter said. "Be there by six o'clock."

"Six o'clock?" Sean asked. "But school doesn't start until eight-thirty, and anyway, tomorrow's Saturday."

"Kid, you'll need to be dressed in costume and through with makeup by seven-fifteen," Miss Carter told him.

Makeup? Yuck! Sean hadn't counted on having to wear makeup.

Miss Carter chuckled. "Don't look so miserable. Even the stars turn out that early." She handed him a card. "Report to Maria. She'll be in one of the trailers."

The next morning Sean had no trouble waking up. He was so excited he was sure he hadn't slept all night. His dad delivered him to the school grounds and helped him find Maria's trailer among the more than twenty huge trucks and trailers that were parked all over the east side of the playground and street.

Dozens of people were setting up equipment near the stairs leading to the east door. Some people were drinking steaming cups of coffee and eating doughnuts, and some were shouting orders. There were also lots of people standing around watching.

"It's a cloudy day," Sean said to his dad. "If there isn't enough sun, does that mean they won't have enough light to film the movie?"

"Movie companies use lights powerful enough to be sunshine," Mr. Quinn said. "They won't have any problems."

Sean stopped and gawked as a man yelled to two of the crew members who were carrying potted plants, "Put them on the right side of the steps!"

They did, and he yelled, "Now try them on the left side. . . . No. Take them away. Wait . . . put them by the side wall. Where's that autographed basketball? Okay. It belongs on the lower step."

"Come on, Sean. You've got an appointment," Mr. Quinn said. He led Sean to Maria's trailer.

"Hi, Sean," Maria said with a smile. "They

sent your costume over here. You can go in that back room and put it on."

She held out a pair of jeans, a white T-shirt, and a San Francisco Forty-niners jacket. Sean, who'd been wondering what kind of weird costume he might have to wear, gave a sigh of relief. "Cool," he said.

He said good-bye to his dad, put on the costume, and reported back to Maria.

She put him into a chair that faced a mirror surrounded by lights. Then she tucked small towels around his neck to protect his clothing and got to work.

Sean made a face as she put a creamy foundation on his face. "Guys don't wear makeup," he complained.

"Sure they do, when they're acting," she said.

"I bet Dakota Wayne doesn't."

Maria chuckled and pointed to some special jars on a nearby shelf. "Yes he does. That's Dakota's special makeup. He's got a lot of allergies. It's hereditary on his father's side. Anyhow, Dakota's allergic to something in the usual creams and face powder we use, so we always have his own personal makeup on hand."

Sean closed his eyes and let Maria get to work. She had almost finished when someone poked his head inside the trailer door and said, "Hurry up. Sean's wanted on the set."

Sean's heart gave a jump. *Wanted on the set.* Wow! Even though he was just a stand-in, he had a part in making a movie!

"Follow me," Maria said, and she walked from the trailer. Sean was right behind her.

But someone yelled, "Watch out!" and Sean and Maria were shoved out of the way.

With a loud crash, one of the tall light standards smashed to the ground—right where they had been standing.

Brian, Sam, and some of the kids on the basketball team ran to Sean.

"What happened?" Sean asked.

"I saw the light start to fall," Brian said. "It was weird. It didn't fall like it was top-heavy. It just fell."

"Like it was pushed," Sam said.

"Yeah," Brian answered. "And it fell in a spot that had emptied, like someone had planned it. At least it was empty until you and Maria got in the way."

"I don't care how it happened. We can't afford any more problems," a tall, skinny man said. He shook his head so hard his ponytail bounced.

"Who's he?" Sean asked.

"I heard people calling him Max. He's one of the assistant directors," Brian answered.

A short, small-boned man standing next to Max said, "If I were you I'd get rid of the grip responsible for that light. I think you should fire him. That will show people there's no jinx. It was the grip's fault."

"You're probably right," Max said. "We can't survive any more of these rumors about a jinx."

Debbie Jean wailed in Sean's ear, "The picture can't be jinxed! Being in a movie—a movie with Dakota Wayne—is the most important thing I've ever done in my whole life!"

A small, mousy-haired woman rushed up. She clutched the arm of a blond boy dressed exactly like Sean.

"What happened? What was that crash?" she called to Max.

As Max began to explain, Sean turned to the boy. "Hi," he said. "You're Justin Moore, aren't you?"

Justin looked at the way Sean was dressed and smiled. "Yes, I am. You must be my stand-in."

"Yeah," Sean said. "I'm Sean Quinn."

"Hi, Sean," Justin said. "I hope you don't mind all the boring stuff that goes on when you're making a movie." He took a quick look around. Then he pulled a candy bar out of his pocket and stuffed most of it into his mouth.

Sean was surprised. "It hasn't been boring so far," he said. "With that light crashing down and—"

"The jinx," Sam interrupted.

Justin looked scared. He gulped down the last bite of candy as he said, "I know about the jinx. Don't talk about it!"

"There's no jinx," Sean said. "At least that's what my dad said. Sam just—" Sean didn't get a chance to finish. A hand gripped his shoulder. "Come with me," Maria said. "Hurry. They want you on the set."

Sean followed Maria to a nearby spot that had been marked with a small piece of colored tape. Maria combed Sean's hair again and once more powdered his nose, making him sneeze.

Max positioned Sean and said, "Stand right where you are. Don't move."

Sean stood still as the broken light was replaced. Many lights, with different kinds of filters, were focused on him. Reflectors were added.

A camera operator called, "Gaffer, get that shadow off the lower side of his face." Reflectors and lights were rearranged and focused again.

"I don't like the potted plants there. They have to be moved," Max called. He took a step forward. "Hey! Where's the basketball?"

"I dunno," somebody shouted back. "I put it on the lower step, just like I was told to."

"We need that basketball in the shot," Max insisted. "You've got to find it."

"Can't I just get another basketball?"

"No, you can't. This one's got autographs all over it. There's not another one like it."

"Is it valuable?"

"It's valuable because it's part of the script and part of the set." Max's face grew red. "We left Hollywood to get away from problems like broken equipment and disappearing props. I don't want any more excuses. Find that basketball!"

"Right away," a crew member said, and hurried off.

The camera operator called to a gaffer again, and the lights and reflectors were moved to other positions. Sean shifted from one foot to the other and yawned.

"Hold still, Sean," someone ordered.

At that moment Sean saw Dakota Wayne walk into the school yard. Dakota was tall with black hair and blue eyes and looked much older than he had in his last picture. He was surrounded by a large group of studio people, including the short man who had wanted the studio grip fired. Sean stretched for a better look as he saw Debbie Jean squeal and run toward Dakota.

A cameraman yelled, "Stop moving around, kid! You've got to stand still!"

"But Dakota just got here," Sean protested. "I want to see him."

"That's not your job. We've got to film him

pretty soon, so stop wasting our time," the cameraman said.

Sean tried not to move. He couldn't see anything, but he could hear. Nearby, Mrs. Moore said in a low voice, "Justin, darling, it doesn't matter how much fuss they're making over Dakota Wayne. *You're* going to be the real star of this film, not Dakota."

Justin answered, "Get real, Mom. They're all hanging around Dakota, not around me."

"Give it time," she said. "You're an up-and-coming young actor with a great future, while Dakota's outgrowing his child roles and will soon be a has-been."

"Aw, Mom, don't talk like that," Justin grumbled. "I like Dakota."

"Maybe so, but just wait and see. You'll find out your mother is right," she said smugly.

Sean wanted to turn and stare, but he

didn't dare move. What was Mrs. Moore talking about? If it concerned the accidents and burglaries that were happening on the set, then maybe she was a part of it.

D EBBIE JEAN GAVE a happy squeal, and Sean turned to see what was going on. But Max stopped him with a yell. "Sean Quinn, you were told not to move!"

Sean's excitement about being a stand-in for Justin Moore quickly faded. The lights were hot; he wasn't allowed to move; and when he absolutely couldn't stand it any longer and scratched his nose, one of Maria's assistants rushed out of nowhere and powdered it again. That made it itch even more.

Finally, the people around the cameras and lights seemed to agree about everything. Justin moved out of the crowd and walked to where Sean was standing. Justin was scarfing down another candy bar.

"I see what you meant about boring," Sean told him.

"It's just as bad for the actors," Justin said. "We say a few lines, then have to say them over and over and over again."

"What if you get them right the first time?"

"I do get them right the first time. My mother sees to that. But the director wants to try them one way, then another way, then—"

A woman wearing huge, very dark sunglasses took Sean's arm. "C'mon, kid, out of the way," she said, and pulled him off the set.

"But I want to talk to Justin," Sean told her.

"Not now. No way," the woman said, but her voice softened. "You can stand back here and watch, if you want."

People hurried around the set, straightening things and picking up almost invisible items. Maria kept powdering Justin's face and smoothing his hair.

A crew member ran in with the basketball and put it into position. "Found it in a trash can!" he yelled.

"Who'd do a dumb thing like putting it in a trash can?" Max yelled, but he glared at the kids on the Redoaks Junior High basketball team.

"Hey, we didn't—," Sam started to say, but Max turned his back and stared into a viewfinder on one of the cameras.

A large, sunburned man, who was dressed in a white T-shirt and jeans, walked onto the set and squatted next to Justin. "In this scene you're talking to your big brother," he said. "You've heard he's running with the wrong crowd in his sixth-grade class, and you're worried about him. When you say your line I want to see some real concern on your face. Okay?"

"Okay, Mr. Hightower," Justin said.

So that's Frank Hightower, the famous director, Sean thought.

Mr. Hightower left Justin and sat in a director's chair in front of a computer. On the chair's canvas back was printed FRANK HIGHTOWER.

Mr. Hightower gave a cue, and the assistant director called, "Places up, please. Rehearsal. Quiet all around."

Throughout the large group of people working on the film others yelled, like an echo, "Quiet! . . . Quiet! . . . Quiet!"

Justin stepped onto the piece of colored tape, and Mr. Hightower walked over to him, talking quietly about what he wanted Justin to do.

Justin nodded, and Mr. Hightower walked

back to his chair. "Rehearsal up!" he called.

The other voices called, "Rehearsal up! . . . Rehearsing! . . . Quiet!"

On cue, Justin looked at a spot at the head of the stairs and talked to an invisible character. "What's wrong?" he asked.

"Good. Let's do it again," Mr. Hightower said. "This time look just a little more worried."

Justin went through the scene again and again.

Sean edged closer to Maria. "Is this a ghost story? Is Justin talking to something nobody sees?"

Maria shook her head. "In this scene Justin's talking to his big brother, but these are close-up shots of Justin. The director doesn't want to waste Dakota's time by using him anywhere he can't be seen. He'll shoot Dakota by himself, then do the long shots with the boys together."

Finally Mr. Hightower called for the scene to be filmed. Maria rushed to Justin with her comb and powder puff, and his mother straightened his shirt collar.

"Roll tape. Camera," the assistant director called.

Someone from the sound department, who worked at a machine filled with windows and dials, called back, "Speed."

"That means the sound tape is ready," Maria whispered.

"Action!" Mr. Hightower called.

Sean watched as a digital clapboard, with information about the scene, the take, the date, and other stuff, was snapped in front of Justin's face.

A camera and seated cameraman rode on a dolly with thick, silent rubber wheels, which was slowly pushed forward. Justin went through the scene. Then he did it again. Five times. Or was it six? Sean yawned.

"Good work, Justin," Mr. Hightower said. "That's a wrap. Next, we'll—"

Mr. Hightower was interrupted as a cluster of people arrived and surrounded him.

Brian and Sam stepped up next to Sean. "That was it?" Brian asked. "All that setup and waiting for less than thirty seconds of film?"

Mr. Hightower suddenly jumped to his feet. "Great! Just great!" he yelled. "It's only time and money. Didn't anyone think this through before firing the guy?"

Max answered, "If the grip was responsible for the falling light standard . . ."

"He says he wasn't. Get him back on the set. On top of everything else, we can't afford a work strike." Mr. Hightower grimaced and rubbed his fingers through his hair. "All right, people," he yelled. "We're taking an hour break. Hopefully, we'll settle our current problem by then."

Justin, munching on another candy bar, stepped in between Sam and Brian. He looked up at Sam and said, "You talked about a jinx. Tell me more about it."

Brian smiled as he interrupted. "Sam is full of scary stories. Don't pay any attention to him."

Justin didn't smile back. He wiped the back of his hand across the chocolate smear on his mouth and said, "Tell me. I want to know."

Sam shrugged. "It's just that bad things keep happening on the set of *New Guy in Town*, so some people think that—"

"Some people who are dumb and super-stitious," Brian interrupted.

"There's no jinx," Sean said, although he

honestly couldn't help wondering.

"I think there is," Sam said in his spooky voice.

Someone, hurrying past, shoved soft drinks into everyone's hands. Sean and Brian automatically said, "Thanks," but neither of them looked up to see who'd given them the ice-cold cans.

"Cut out the scary stuff, Sam," Brian said.

"Yeah. Accidents happen," Sean said.

Justin sighed. "My mother told me this film is my big chance. I don't want to lose it because of a jinx."

"It's my big chance, too!" Debbie Jean squeezed into the group.

Mrs. Moore's voice rang out. "Justin? Where are you?"

"I gotta go," Justin said.

He looked so unhappy that Sean blurted

out, "Hey, after you're through today, why don't you meet me here on the playground. My friends Matt and Jabez and some of the other kids are going to get together and play baseball. You can play any position you want."

"I've never played baseball," Justin said. "Thanks for asking me, though. After filming I have to do my schoolwork and learn my lines for the next day. I work until bedtime."

"Justin!" Mrs. Moore shouted.

"Gotta go," Justin said, and he ran to join his mother.

Maria joined the group. "I heard you talking about the jinx," she said. "I didn't believe it at first, but now I do. Everything has been going wrong. That's proof there's a jinx, isn't it?"

Brian shook his head. "It's more likely that someone's just trying to make everyone believe that the film is jinxed."

"Nobody has to pretend there's a jinx when a whole series of crazy things happen to *prove* there's a jinx," Maria said.

Brian tossed his empty soft drink can into one of the large trash cans that stood nearby. Then he pulled out his notepad and pencil. "Have you been with the company right from the start of *New Guy in Town*?" he asked Maria.

"It depends on what you mean when you say, 'right from the start,'" Maria answered. "I was signed to supervise makeup as soon as the story was set to film."

"Then you wouldn't have been there when the head scriptwriter quit. You wouldn't know what caused the problem," Brian said.

"I wasn't there, but I know," Maria said. "Everybody talked about it. The head script-writer quit because of Ralph Wayne. He's Dakota Wayne's father and also his business manager. Mr. Wayne kept insisting on changes. Then he said that the whole script was bad and would ruin his son's career. He demanded a new writer and a new script."

A sudden scream caused Sean to jump and drop his soft drink can. The workers and sight-seers on the set froze, staring as Mrs. Moore ran out of her trailer. "Help! Please help!" she cried. "Justin's been poisoned! Somebody call 9-1-1!"

M<small>R</small>. H<small>IGHTOWER RAN</small> to the Moores' trailer, while at least a dozen people pulled cellular phones from their belts and dialed.

Brian took one look at Sean's spilled soft drink and said, "That may be it!"

"What's it?"

"I haven't got time to tell you now. Hurry up, Sean! We've got to make sure that—"

"Sure of what?" Sean asked, but he ran with Brian to the trailer.

It took a while to squeeze through the crowd that had formed outside the trailer's door.

Then, when they made it, one of the grips blocked the door. "Outta the way," he ordered Brian.

"I just want to get—"

"Look out!" someone called as the paramedics appeared. The crowds of people parted, and Brian and Sean were pushed aside.

In just a few minutes the paramedics reappeared, carrying Justin on a stretcher.

As the crowd inside the trailer followed the paramedics to the ambulance, Brian whispered to Sean, "Stay here!" He disappeared into the trailer. Within two minutes he came out, holding a soft drink can wrapped in a paper towel.

Sean's eyes widened, and he clutched his throat. "That's the stuff we were all drinking!"

"Don't look so scared. You weren't poisoned," Brian said.

"What are you going to do with that can?"

"Give it to one of the police. There are some police cars over there."

Sean glanced in the direction Brian was looking. "Detective Kerry just drove up."

Brian gave the soft drink can to Detective Kerry and explained that Justin had been drinking from it. "There's still some of the drink left in the can," he said, "in case you want to test it."

"We certainly do want to test it," Detective Kerry said. "Good thinking, Brian."

The short, small-boned man who Sean and Brian had seen earlier walked up to Mr. Hightower, who was standing nearby. The short man had his arm around Dakota Wayne's shoulders.

"He's always around Dakota," Sean whispered. "He must be Dakota's father."

"Frank, the limo's arrived," the man said to Mr. Hightower. "Dakota and I are leaving."

"Leaving? What are you talking about, Ralph?" Mr. Hightower's voice kept rising as he spoke. "You can't leave! The break's only for one hour, and then we'll be ready to film Dakota. The paramedics told us that Justin's vital signs are good. He's got a stomachache but he doesn't show signs of having been poisoned. It may be one of those twenty-four-hour bugs. Also, we're rehiring the grip so there won't be a strike. Production's already way behind schedule. You can't—"

"Frank, you must understand our position," Ralph Wayne said. "As Dakota's father, I'm extremely concerned for his health. If there's even a small chance that someone's poisoning the cast of *New Guy in Town*, then I can't allow my son to remain on the set, where he'll be in danger. Dakota's much too valuable."

Dakota said, "Dad, nothing's going to happen to me. You just heard Mr. Hightower tell us Justin didn't show any signs of being poisoned. I'd like to stay."

Mr. Wayne shook his head. "No, Dakota. We're leaving."

Mr. Hightower's face grew red. He shouted, "No matter what, you'd better have Dakota here on the set on time Monday, or I'll file a complaint with the Screen Actors Guild and make a lot of noise with the press. As you well know, a kid who's difficult to work with will find it hard to get jobs!"

"We'll see about that," Mr. Wayne grumbled. He grabbed Dakota's arm and marched out of the school yard and to the curb, where a long black limousine stood waiting.

Mr. Hightower sank into his chair with a groan. Finally, he raised his head and said, "Max, tell everyone that production will be shut down for the rest of the day. Tell them to report back to the set Monday morning at six."

"Uh-oh," Maria said. "That's a big surprise. It costs an awful lot of money to shut down a set."

"But neither of the stars are here," Sean said.

"Max could take the shots they need of the extras and the background," Maria said. She shrugged. "Oh, well, it doesn't matter to me. I get a paid afternoon off."

* * *

ON THE LOCAL five o'clock news the top story was Justin Moore's illness. There had been no signs of poisoning, and Justin was now feeling fine, but his doctors decided to keep him overnight for observation.

The story of Justin's illness even made a national entertainment television show. Justin's mother was interviewed and spoke of her son's brave desire to return to work to save the film, in spite of his illness.

Detective Kerry dropped by to see the Quinns, just as the newscast had finished. "I thought you boys would like to know that nothing had been put in Justin's soft drink," he said to Brian and Sean. "We checked the can for fingerprints, but there were too many, and most were smudged."

"I wonder why Justin got so sick that his mother would think he was poisoned?" Sean asked. "I hope it doesn't happen to him again. If the movie isn't made, he'll be out a lot of money."

"No, he won't," Detective Kerry said. "I was told that the major actors, the director, and the cinematographer have pay-or-play contracts. That means they'll get paid even if the movie is never made."

"Wow!" Sean said.

"Unless, of course, a natural disaster is responsible, like an earthquake or a hurricane."

Sean groaned and promised himself to catch a look at the local weather report. All sorts of crazy things had gone wrong. All Donner Productions needed now was a volcanic eruption or a tornado!

6

IN A FEW MINUTES, Debbie Jean came over. "Come on in the kitchen," she said to Sean and Brian. "We need to talk."

Sean made a face. Debbie Jean was the bossiest person he'd ever met. She always wanted to take over. "Whose house is this, anyway?" Sean muttered.

"If you don't know, you're in real trouble," Debbie Jean said, and giggled. She plopped down in one of the chairs at the kitchen table and said, "My grandfather gave me twenty dollars for my birthday, so I want to hire you."

Sean stopped wrinkling his nose as though

he smelled something terrible, and looked surprised. "For what?" he asked.

Closing her eyes and holding the back of one hand to her forehead, Debbie Jean sighed dramatically. "I want to be in this movie. I *have* to be in this movie," she said. "It's my big chance."

"What big chance?" Sean scoffed. "You're only an extra."

"That's better than being a stand-in," she snapped. "At least *my* face will be in *front* of the camera." She slapped a twenty-dollar bill on the table in front of Brian. "You and Sean are the Casebusters. You solve cases," she said. "So solve this one. Find out who's trying to make people think this film is jinxed—besides Sam. Save this movie!"

Sean reached for the twenty, but Brian was faster. He grabbed it and shoved it back at Debbie Jean. "My partner and I will take this case," he said, "but keep your money."

Sean picked up the money as he said, "We may have expenses. Make that, we *will* have expenses."

"Nothing we need to charge for. Give back the money," Brian told Sean.

"But—"

Debbie Jean snatched the money from Sean and stuffed it into the pocket of her jeans. "I'm ready. Let's talk business," she said.

Brian pulled out his notebook and looked from Debbie Jean to Sean. "Okay. We'll begin by writing down what we found out about some of the people connected with this film," he said. "I'll start with the notes I made about Dakota's father, Ralph Wayne. According to what Maria told us, he's the one who didn't like the first script and caused so many problems that the head scriptwriter was fired."

Debbie Jean said, "Put down Frank High-tower. His last two movies flopped. I over-heard someone say that Mr. Hightower wants to start his own production company and make adventure movies. What if he wants out of this movie he's unhappy with so he can make films with his own company?"

Brian shook his head. "From everything we've heard, Mr. Hightower really needs this movie to build his reputation again. You saw how he nearly came apart when everything went wrong today."

Sean nodded agreement and said, "He closed down the set awfully quick. Remember, Maria told us it costs a lot of money to close down a set."

"Put down Justin Moore's name," Debbie Jean said. "He could have faked being poi-soned to get publicity."

"That's dumb," Sean said.

"No it isn't," Debbie Jean said. "He got lots of publicity. So did his mother."

"Justin's not like that," Sean said. "He's a nice guy."

Brian said, "Our first step is just to list the possible suspects. Then we start collecting information and eliminating the ones who don't seem to be guilty." He wrote more notes before he added, "We've got to think about the whole series of problems the film company has had. I don't think that Justin and his mother could have pulled them all off."

"But I heard that Mrs. Moore wants her son to be the star of the film, not Dakota Wayne," Debbie Jean said.

Sean gulped. He'd actually heard Mrs. Moore say something like that to Justin. But Sean refused to admit that Justin had a part in any of this. He said, "Mrs. Moore wouldn't do anything to hurt her son or his character."

Sean grinned evilly at Debbie Jean. "Anyway, how about Dakota Wayne? I got the idea, from things his dad said, that Dakota would like to get out of the film. He doesn't enjoy playing kids anymore."

"Don't say anything against Dakota Wayne," Debbie Jean warned. "He's gorgeous. He's wonderful. He gave me his autograph."

But Brian kept writing. "Okay, so he's wonderful and maybe he can even wiggle his ears, but we're trying to solve a case," he said. "Right now, everyone on that set's a suspect."

"Not Maria," Sean said.

"Sure. Even Maria."

Although Debbie Jean scowled at him, Brian went on taking notes. "Tiffany told me that Dakota is wealthy," he said. "Because of his father's business investments, he's set for life. He doesn't have to make this movie."

Sean remembered the pay-and-play clause. "Yeah. And even if the movie folds, Dakota will get paid."

"Okay. We're all agreed? Dakota's a suspect and so is his dad," Brian said.

"How come?" Debbie Jean asked stubbornly.

"Dakota's playing the part of a little kid in *New Guy in Town*," Brian explained. "And he's not a little kid anymore. If the film critics and the public think he's miscast, the movie will probably bomb. It won't help Dakota's career if his newest movie is a flop."

"Don't forget Max. He blamed the grip for knocking over the light and fired him," Sean said.

"He's not completely to blame. We were there. We heard Dakota's father talking the assistant director into firing the guy," Brian answered.

"You've got a lot of names and information written down," Debbie Jean said, "but it doesn't tell you who's jinxing the movie. How are you going to find out?"

"By narrowing our list down until we come to the one person who has the motive and the means."

"What does that mean?"

"Somebody badly wants that film shut down for what he—or she—thinks are good reasons. That's the *motive*. And somebody was able to be on hand when each of the problems took place. That's the *means*."

"Can you do it?"

"We're the Casebusters, aren't we?" Sean bragged, but he couldn't help wondering how they were going to come up with the answers.

7

AFTER DINNER THAT evening, Brian and Sean rode their bikes to the hospital to see Justin.

A nurse at the desk shook her head. "We're supposed to see that Justin doesn't have too many visitors," she said.

A grandmotherly nurse stepped up and smiled. "I think we can make an exception here. Justin's feeling lonely and unhappy. I'm sure that he'd like to talk to boys his own age, not just grown-ups."

The other nurse shrugged, and Brian said, "Thanks."

"Justin's mother just went down to the cafeteria," the older nurse said. "I'll take you to his room."

Justin lay sunk in pillows, looking bored. But he smiled and sat up in bed as Sean and Brian came into the room.

"Hi, Sean," he said.

"Hi," Sean said. "This is my brother, Brian. You were talking to him earlier, but I didn't get a chance to introduce you. Brian's an extra in your movie. We came to see how you were feeling."

"And to ask if you know who gave you the soft drink," Brian said.

"But Detective Kerry said—," Sean began. He stopped when Brian frowned at him.

Justin shrugged. "I don't know who gave us the drinks. We were all talking, and then the drinks were handed out. I wasn't paying attention." He thought a moment. "Why? What does it matter?"

"Just curious," Brian said.

Justin hugged his arms and drew back against the pillows. His eyes were wide and scared. "Was it the drink that made me sick?" he whispered. "Did somebody put something in it?"

"Detective Kerry tested the drink," Brian said. "He told us that nothing had been put in it."

"Then why did you ask about it?"

"I just wanted to make sure," Brian said. Justin looked so miserable that Brian tried to cheer him up. "Hey, look. It's all over. There's nothing to be scared about."

Justin didn't look cheered up. He looked even worse. "Something's wrong isn't it?" he whispered. "I was on the steps to our trailer

when the light standard fell. I saw it go over."
He shivered. "It's the jinx, isn't it?"

"No," Brian said. "Take our word for it. There's
no jinx. There's just someone who wants this
movie to fail, and we're going to stop him."

"How?" Justin asked.

"We don't know yet, but we will. Trust us.
We're private investigators. We call ourself the
Casebusters, and we've managed to solve all
kinds of cases."

Justin managed a smile. "Okay, Casebusters,"
he said. "Go for it."

Sean pulled a slightly squashed candy
bar out of his pocket and handed it to
Justin. "Here," he said. "I brought you a
present."

"You shouldn't have brought him candy.
They won't let him eat it," Brian said. "He has
to eat the hospital food."

"Hospital food is yucky. I remember from when I had my tonsils out. That's why I thought Justin would like a candy bar," Sean said.

Justin grinned at Sean and tore at the wrapper. "Thanks. I love candy," he said. "My mom only lets me eat what she calls *healthy foods*, so she never allows me to eat candy."

The nurse came into Justin's room, and he slipped the opened candy bar under the sheet. "Time to leave, boys," the nurse said. She shooed them out into the hall just as Mrs. Moore stepped out of the elevator.

Mrs. Moore hurried past and into Justin's room, as though she didn't really see Brian and Sean. But just as Brian and Sean reached the elevators, they heard Mrs. Moore let out an angry shout.

"Oh-oh. She found the candy bar," Sean said. The elevator doors opened and he jumped inside the elevator. He hoped Justin wouldn't tell her where the candy came from. He didn't want someone as nervous and excitable as Mrs. Moore to get mad at him.

A s Brian and Sean left the hospital, Brian said, "Let's ride home past your school."

"Why? Nobody will be there at night," Sean said.

"That's the point," Brian explained. "The equipment trucks and trailers are parked on the school grounds, and nobody should be around, except maybe for a watchman."

"You mean, we're going to take a look and see if someone's there who shouldn't be?" Sean asked.

"Right," Brian said.

"What if the watchman chases us away?"

"We'll see what happens when we get there," Brian said.

As Brian and Sean rounded the last corner on their bikes, the school building loomed up ahead of them, its darkened windows like rows of closed eyelids.

Far beyond the building, near the outer fence, however, a light flickered, then went out. Brian and Sean braked quickly.

"Did you see that light?" Brian whispered.

"I think it was in one of the trailers," Sean answered.

"Third from the right," Brian said. "Look! There it is again."

"Uh-oh. That's Maria's makeup trailer," Sean said. He sneaked a hopeful look at Brian. "Of course, it could be the night watchman."

"Let's find out," Brian said. He led the way

to the main gate and found it padlocked.

"We can't get in here," he said. "Ride around to the back."

Slowly, cautiously, they did. The streetlight at the corner lit only a small area, so the low, wide-spreading branches of the trees along the street created a dark tunnel. Brian and Sean rested their bikes against a tree and took off their helmets.

The lights flickered again, and Sean gave a sigh of relief. "Look, Bri! It's nowhere near Maria's trailer."

"Maybe it *is* a night watchman," Brian said.

Sean looked over his shoulder at the creepy blackness. "Okay. Good. Let's go home."

"Not until we're sure," Brian said. He walked to the fence and along it until he suddenly stopped and held out an arm to stop Sean from going any farther.

"Ooof!" Sean walked right into Brian's arm.

"Be quiet!" Brian whispered. "I hear some-one."

A voice spoke so close by that both Brian and Sean jumped.

"I've got it," a man's voice said. "I was right. It must have fallen out of my pocket."

A woman answered, "Good," and Sean and Brian immediately recognized her voice—Maria.

"I gave you that little pocketknife," Maria said. "I would have been unhappy if you'd lost it." She paused, and her voice became quiet and serious as she asked, "Max, were you in my trailer?"

"In your trailer?" Max answered. "Of course not. Why do you ask?"

"Because I think someone was in the trailer. While I was waiting for you a few moments ago,

I decided to check out my trailer. The minute I was inside the door I saw that things were slightly out of place. There was a magazine on the floor, and I'm sure I left it on a table by the doorway. A bottle of hand lotion had moved a few inches from where I always keep it. There were a few other little things like that."

"Had anything been taken?" Max asked.

"No. I double-checked. I don't keep anything valuable in the trailer, which is why I usually don't lock it."

"This time, lock it," Max said.

As the voices moved farther away, Brian said, "Let's get out of here. We don't want them to see us. They'll think we've been spying on them."

"Well, haven't we?" Sean asked.

"Not exactly," Brian answered. "Private investigators call it *surveillance*."

"How did they get in, and how are they going to get out?" Sean asked.

"Max seems to be in charge of a lot of things. He probably has a key to the padlock," Brian answered.

"Then it seems to me that Max has the means," Sean said.

"Maybe so," Brian said. He wheeled his bike out into the street, and Sean followed, heading for home.

*   *   *

LATE THAT EVENING Brian and Sean sat on the edge of Brian's bed while Brian finished writing in his notebook.

"I may be wrong," Brian told Sean, "but the way it looks to me we can narrow the suspects down to the only three people who seem to have both motive and means: Frank Hightower, Ralph Wayne, and Dakota Wayne."

"What about Maria and Max?"

"Max would have been hired about the same time Maria was," Brian said. "Neither one of them would have been with the production company when the trouble started."

"Yeah," Sean said. "I remember. Maria said she wasn't hired until the production company was ready to shoot the film."

"That's right," Brian said, "and I can't see that she'd have any kind of motive."

"Then what was she doing on the empty set tonight?" Sean asked.

"I'm guessing that she came to keep Max company while he looked for his pocketknife."

"If that's what he was really doing," Sean said.

"Do you think he was lying to Maria?"

"I don't know. He could have been."

"We don't have proof one way or another,"

Brian said. "Why don't we go through the rest of our list?"

"Okay," Sean said. "How about Mrs. Moore?"

Brian shook his head. "She wasn't on the set either, until filming began, so she didn't have the means. And she wants her son to look good in the film, so I don't think she has a motive, either. Just like I said, I think the person causing all the problems is either Frank Hightower, Dakota Wayne, or Ralph Wayne."

"How are we going to find out which one it is?" Sean asked. "And, even if we know, how are we going to prove it?"

"The culprit won't be through causing trouble until the film is totally shut down, with no hopes of it being made," Brian said. "So we get ready for the next disaster to take place on the set."

A shiver ran up Sean's backbone. "What disaster are you talking about? Is it going to be anything that could hurt somebody? I'm allergic to disasters!"

Brian put a reassuring hand on Sean's shoulder. "No one's been hurt . . . so far," he said. "When the set caught on fire, no one was there. When the light fell, no one was supposed to be in its path."

"But next time . . ."

"Don't worry about the next time," Brian grinned. "Thanks to something you just said, Sean, I have a pretty good idea of what's going to happen next. And I think I know who's going to cause it. All we have to do is be there when it happens."

9

EARLY MONDAY MORNING, when Sean and Brian arrived on the set, Dakota was already seated in the big chair in Maria's makeup trailer. Ralph Wayne, his hands jammed into his pockets, stood a few feet away with Frank Hightower. Their heads were close together, and they spoke quietly. Some of the crew worked nonstop, setting up lights and reflectors and rolling the heavier cameras into position. A lot of people seemed to just stand around, watching.

"Hi," Dakota said, when he saw Sean and Brian in the open doorway. "Come on in."

"I didn't think you'd be here so early," Sean said. "I thought it would be like Saturday, when Justin was first."

Dakota rubbed his chin, but Maria pushed his hand away and repowdered the spot. "Dad told Mr. Hightower that Justin should get as much rest as he could. He volunteered to have me do some of my scenes first."

"That was very thoughtful of your father," Maria said.

Sean wished someone had thought of telling Justin's stand-in that he could stay in bed late, too. He yawned.

Maria smiled at Sean. "Check with Max for your schedule for today, Sean. You'll probably be free to go back to school this morning."

She whipped off the makeup cape that covered Dakota's clothes and escorted him out the door.

"Stop rubbing your ear," she told Dakota.

"It itches," Dakota complained.

Maria took a good look at his face. Then she gasped and peered even closer. "Uh-oh!" she said.

Puffy red blotches were beginning to spread all over Dakota's face, ears, and neck.

"Dad," Dakota said. "That rash . . . that allergy . . . I've got it again."

Sean barely realized that Brian had jumped up and gone to Maria's makeup stand. He was more concerned about Mr. Wayne, whose face grew so angry it turned the color of tomato soup.

"Look at Dakota!" he bellowed at Frank Hightower. "He's a mess! You can't film him like this! I'm taking him off the set—for good!"

"You can't. I told you—," Mr. Hightower began, but Ralph Wayne was louder.

He jammed his hands even more deeply

into his pockets and yelled, "It doesn't matter what you told me. This isn't my fault! And it isn't Dakota's fault!"

Maria gasped. "It's the jinx!"

"Maybe you're the jinx, Maria," Mr. Wayne snapped. "You're to blame! How could you be so careless?"

Brian stepped up and joined them. "Don't blame Maria," he said. "Someone switched Dakota's allergy-free makeup with the kind he's allergic to."

"Only Maria could have done that," Mr. Wayne insisted.

Brian shook his head. "It will be easy to find out. I wrapped the jars and put them into a paper bag. The police will probably get fingerprints from them, and that will tell us who was handling the jars."

"Don't play detective," Mr. Wayne said. He

hunched over, his hands still in his pockets. "I want those jars thrown out. Get them away from here so they can't contaminate Dakota." He glared at one of the nearby crew members. "Get those jars," he ordered. "Dispose of them—now!"

"I wouldn't if I were you," Brian told the crew member. "I've already labeled them for the police. Detective Kerry won't like it if someone disposes of evidence."

The crew member stopped and stepped away from the trailer.

"All the evidence we need is on poor Dakota's face," Mr. Wayne insisted.

"And on one other place," Brian said. "You have the same allergy to the makeup, Mr. Wayne. You would have had to touch the makeup to put it into Dakota's special makeup jars. I think that's why you've been keeping your hands in your pockets. They probably look as red and blotchy as Dakota's face."

"Nonsense!" Mr. Wayne snapped.

"Dad?" Dakota stared in horror at his father.

Frank Hightower yanked at Ralph Wayne's right arm. "Prove it to us!" Mr. Hightower yelled. "Let's see your hands."

"I'm not going to let you . . ." Mr. Wayne twisted away so fast that he tripped over the heavy electrical cords leading to the lights on the set. To catch his balance and keep from falling, his hands flew out of his pockets.

Sean stared. Just as Brian had said, Mr. Wayne's hands were red and blotchy.

"Dad! You did this?" Dakota said. He groaned. "You'd go this far to get your own way?"

"I did it for you, Dakota!" Mr. Wayne cringed as he looked from Dakota to Mr.

Hightower. "I had to do something!" he whined. "This picture is going to ruin Dakota's career. You have him playing a twelve-year-old, and look at him—he's a tall teenager!"

"Oh, yes!" Debbie Jean said as she stepped up beside Sean. Her eyes shone as she added, "A truly gorgeous tall teenager!"

"Yuck," Sean muttered and moved a foot away from Debbie Jean.

Mr. Wayne clapped his hands over his forehead and moaned. "Audiences will be laughing at Dakota and at you, Frank Hightower. Your career's going to go down the drain, and there's nothing you can do about it."

"Sure there is," Sean heard himself say. As everyone turned to stare at him, he gulped and started again. "Change the script. You can keep the same story line. Just put Dakota Wayne in high school. Take him out of those kid clothes."

"Make him real," Brian added. "Give him a girlfriend."

Debbie Jean squealed. "Oh, yes!" She squealed again.

"*Hmm*," Mr. Hightower said. "A new teenage idol? I suppose it could work."

"I like it," Dakota said. He grinned at Brian. "Especially the part about the girlfriend."

"Someone like *me*," Debbie Jean murmured.

Dakota smiled at Debbie Jean.

She sighed, leaned against Sean for support, and tromped on his foot.

Mr. Wayne jiggled up and down with excitement. "Dakota—the new teenage idol! It *will* work. . . . Look," he said to Frank Hightower, "I'll pay for what I cost you."

"You're darned right you will," Mr. Hightower said.

"Then everything's okay. We can move right ahead."

"Not exactly," Brian said. "What about your giving Justin Moore all those candy bars and then a soft drink? You knew he wasn't used to eating candy and he'd get a stomachache."

"It's not my fault that he wolfed down the candy," Mr. Wayne said.

"Aw, Dad, how could you do that?" Dakota said. "Justin's just a little kid. You're going to have to apologize to Justin and to his mother."

"Yeah," Sean said. He couldn't help hoping that if Mrs. Moore got mad enough at Mr. Wayne, she'd forget about the candy bar Sean had given Justin in the hospital.

Mr. Hightower frowned as he thought. "If Mrs. Moore doesn't press criminal charges against you, she might sue you in civil court."

Mr. Wayne looked really scared.

"Why don't we give Justin co-billing with me?" Dakota suggested. "His mother would like that, and maybe she wouldn't be mad at you."

Mr. Wayne's face grew red again. "You want to be only a costar instead of having top billing? Impossible!"

Dakota put a hand on his father's arm. "Not impossible, Dad. Look what you did to the kid. We're going to have to make it up to him big-time."

Mr. Hightower looked surprised. "Dakota, do you mean it? Would you really be willing to share your screen credits on an equal basis with Justin?"

"I mean it," Dakota said. "If we're going to start over, we're going to do it right."

Mr. Hightower paced to the trailer and back again. "Okay, let's get Joe Miller back to rewrite the script. Max, Miller's in Malibu. Call him.

Get one of the attorneys on the Donner Productions staff to take care of changes in the contract. Get the accounting department. Get wardrobe. Get someone to scout new location shots at the high school."

"And a film test for Debbie Jean Parker," Debbie Jean said quickly.

"Yeah, a film test, whatever," Mr. Hightower said. He whirled and pointed a finger in Mr. Wayne's direction. "Ralph, you take Dakota to a doctor immediately and get that rash cleared up."

"Let's see . . . ," Mr. Hightower went on. "We'll take a week to make changes, and then we'll be off and running. Somebody telephone Justin's mother. I want to talk to her. Let's get going! I want action!"

Brian and Sean grinned at each other. "That's a wrap," Sean said. Sean and Brian burst out laughing.

JOAN LOWERY NIXON is a renowned writer of children's mysteries. She is the author of more than eighty books and the only four-time recipient of the prestigious Edgar Allan Poe Award for the best juvenile mystery of the year.

☾

"I was asked by Disney Adventures *magazine if I could write a short mystery. I decided to write about two young boys who help their father, a private investigator, solve crimes. These boys, Brian and Sean, are actually based on my grandchildren, who are the same ages as the characters. My first Casebusters story was a piece about a ghost that haunts an inn. This derives from a legendary Louisiana inn I visited which was allegedly haunted. Later, I learned the owner had made up the entire tale, and I used that angle in the story."* — JOAN LOWERY NIXON